You're the Greatest, Charlie Brown

You're the Greatest,

Charlie Brown

Charles M. Schulz

SCHOLASTIC BOOK SERVICES
NEW YORK · TORONTO · LONDON · AUCKLAND · SYDNEY · TOKYO

ISBN 0-590-31216-2

Copyright © 1979 by United Feature Syndicate, Inc. Produced in association with Lee Mendelson-Bill Melendez TV Production and Charles M. Schulz Creative Associates. Based upon the Lee Mendelson-Bill Melendez television Production "You're the Greatest, Charlie Brown" (© 1979 United Feature Syndicate, Inc.) All rights reserved under International and Pan-American Copyright Conventions. This edition is published by Scholastic Book Services, a division of Scholastic Magazines, Inc., 50 West 44th Street, New York, N.Y. 10036, by arrangement with Random House, Inc.

12 11 10 9 8 7 6 5 4 3 2   0 1 2 3 4 5/8
Printed in the U.S.A.   09

Okay, gang. We have somebody from our school entered in every event for the Junior Olympics—except the decathlon.

I sure don't want to enter that event. You have to compete in *ten* different things. That's too much work.

Hi, everybody.

Boy! Who'd be dumb enough to enter the decathlon?

I'm not going on vacation after all. So now I can enter the track meet. Are there any events left open?

Sure, Charlie Brown. But I don't think you would . . .

You're in luck, Charlie Brown. There's one event left—the decathlon.

It's perfect for you. You don't have to be good at anything in particular. And you just might end up being the next Bruce Jenner!

It's an awful lot of work, Charlie Brown. You have to do a whole lot of training, and you have to compete in ten events.

That's okay, Linus. It'll be worth the work if I can help the team.

HOORAY! You're the greatest, Charlie Brown!

I'm putting you on a strict training program, Chuck. I want you to start with eight laps every day. That's two miles. Then you'll build up to five miles a day.

That's it, Chuck. Lift those knees!

That's pretty good, Charles.

Gotta build up those arms, Chuck. Come on. Hup, hup!

What's so great about lifting two angel-food cakes?

You lifted those weights seven times. You're very strong.

I appreciate your
working out with me,
Snoopy. You must
be exhausted, too.

We're going over the ten events you'll be competing in, Chuck. The first event is the 400-meter dash. I'll show you how. Then it's your turn.

Your form was very good—at first.

Next is the broad jump.

The shot put.

The high jump.

Okay, high jump, here I come.

The fifth and last event of the first day is the 100-meter dash. You've practiced running today, Chuck, so let's go right on to the next event. On the second day you start here with the high hurdles.

Sure you can, Chuck.

I don't think I can do it.

The seventh event is the ol' discus. You have to stay in the ring here when you throw.

That was a very strong attempt.

CRASH

For the eighth event, get ready to fly through the air.

That's enough
for today, Chuck.

I admire your *élan*, Charles.

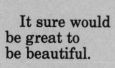
It sure would
be great to
be beautiful.

It sure
would be
great to be
a hero.

Do you think I'm beautiful, Chuck?

Of course, Peppermint Patty.
You have what is sometimes called
a "quiet beauty."

I wish it would speak up now
and then.

Well, enough of this daydreaming.
Back to work!

Congratulations, Charles!

You've been standing here and watching me for days, Marcie. How come?

I thought it would be nice to encourage you, Charles. You've gotten very good. I'm sure you'll do well against Freddy Fabulous.

Freddy Fabulous? He's the all-city champion from last year!

But he's not as good as you— I think. Well, we'll see tomorrow.

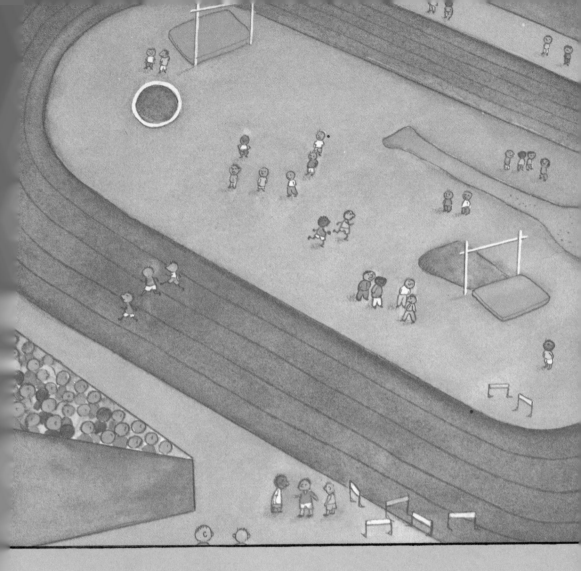

Charlie Brown, if you win your events, our school has a good chance of winning the track meet. So don't blow it!

These are the three competitors you have to worry about. Meet Freddy Fabulous, from Fremont. He won this event last year.

You'll soon be sorry you met me, kid! Ha! Ha! Ha!

I put in Marcie as a backup for our school.

Hmmm. This is strange. I've never heard of *this* school—the Ace Obedience School. Let's see who the person is. . . .

The Masked Marvel!

Event Number 1:
The 400-Meter Dash

Okay, Chuck. Get out there and show them what you're made of!

Hey, that's great!

You did really well, Chuck. You came in last, but your time was good. In the decathlon you get points for your time. So you still have a good chance of catching up.

Event Number 2: The Broad Jump

Ha! Ha! Watch this one, kid!

Don't let him psych you out, Charles. You're better than he is.

Okay, you pigeons. Try and beat that one!

Event Number 3: The Shot Put

Top that one!

Chuck, you took second place in the shot!
Only Freddy Fabulous beat you, and not by much.
You're gonna win the decathlon, Chuck-o!

Event Number 4:
The High Jump

This is my best
event, kids. I'll
snow you under
from here on.

Too bad! Maybe he's getting a little nervous.

Event Number 5: The 100-Meter Dash

Good luck, Marcie.

The Winner By A Nose —
The Masked Marvel!

I don't believe it. After the first five events you're in third place, Charlie Brown. I thought you'd be dead last. Instead, the Masked Marvel is in last place.

You did okay, Chuck, and so did our team. In fact, if you can win the decathlon tomorrow, we may win the Junior Olympics.

I'm so nervous my stomach hurts. The whole school is depending on me.

Don't worry, Charlie Brown. Just try to do your best. Then I'm sure everyone will be satisfied.

Okay, Pumpkin Head, no more nice guy. I'm going to run away from you little kids.

We have a problem, Chuck. The Masked Marvel is
up to you now. We can't afford any more last places.

Event Number 7: The Discus

You did it! You won an
event! You won the discus.

I did?

Stop the world.
I want to get off.

Event Number 8:
The Pole Vault

Chuck, you did very well in the pole vault. Now the four of you are about even.

Event Number 9: The Javelin

Let's see you guys top that one. Ha! Ha! Ha! Ha!

You did it, Chuck! You won the javelin.
You're in first place! All you have to do
is win the final event and you win the
whole thing.

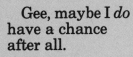

Gee, maybe I *do*
have a chance
after all.

Event Number 10: The 1500-Meter Run

I'm out in front. Maybe I *will* win. I'll be a hero. Wow! They'll treat me like Bruce Jenner . . . parades, flowers . . . Wow!

CHUCK! PAY ATTENTION! OPEN YOUR EYES!

You took the wrong turn!
CHUCK, COME BACK! YOU'RE
OFF THE TRACK!

It's great being a winner—so peaceful and quiet.

I guess the whole school
hates me.

Not to worry, Chuck.
The school won anyway.
Besides, everyone knows
you did your best.

Well, at least I'm glad to hear that
Marcie came out on top.

Hi! I just wanted to congratulate you, Charles, for being such a good sport.

Thanks. And congratulations on winning the decathlon, Marcie.

Thanks, Charles. You're a terrific competitor and a real gentleman. You're the greatest, Charlie Brown!